You're Somebody Special,
WALLIWIGS!

For Niki Daly,
the inspirational force
behind Walliwigs

Also by Joan Rankin

Wow! It's Great Being a Duck
Scaredy Cat
The Little Cat and the Greedy Old Woman
(Margaret K. McElderry Books)

Margaret K. McElderry Books
An imprint of Simon & Schuster Children's Publishing Division
1230 Avenue of the Americas
New York, NY 10020

First published in the United Kingdom by The Bodley Head Children's Books
First U.S. Edition 1999
Printed in Singapore

By arrangement with the Inkman, Cape Town, South Africa
10 9 8 7 6 5 4 3 2 1
Library of Congress Catalog Card Number: 98-65820
· ISBN: 0-689-82230-8

You're Somebody Special,
WALLIWIGS!

E RAN

JOAN RANKIN

MARGARET K. MCELDERRY BOOKS

Walliwigs' mother was a somewhat foolish parrot.
She made her nest in a *very* silly place—
on top of a ship's funnel.

"Walliwigs," said his mother one day, "I'm going for a little fly-about. Now, you are not to *move* from this spot. Do you hear me?"

"Yes, Ma," said Walliwigs.

"Bye bye, Walliwigs!"
"Bye bye, Ma!"

While Walliwigs' mother was enjoying her flight over the Botanical Gardens, the ship started to move. It sailed out of the harbor. Walliwigs could see the sea. It was *very* wide and *very* deep.

All day long, the ship sailed across the big, blue sea. Walliwigs missed his lunch. By suppertime he was ravenous.

"Maaaa, Maaaa! I'm hungry!" cried Walliwigs.

"I want my supper!" He squawked and squawked.

The ship's cook looked out to see what all the fuss was about.

Such a big noise for such a tiny parrot. I couldn't even make pineapple-parrot pie from it.

The Captain came out on the bridge. "Call Sid the ship's boy to get that thing out of my smokestack!"

Sid, the ship's boy, loved climbing up smokestacks, so that was okay.

He also loved his parrot-eating python, Harold.

You're so small and such a BIG nuisance.

But he did not love parrots.

When the ship arrived at the next port, Sid put Walliwigs in a pineapple box and took him ashore to his Aunt Beth.

Oh, Sidney, what have you brought me this time?

Pineapple-parrot pie! That doesn't sound very nice.

When Sid had gone, Aunt Beth wondered what to do with Walliwigs.

The only birds Aunt Beth liked were her chickens. So she put Walliwigs with one of her hens, Martha, and hoped for the best.

"What is this?" said Martha, inspecting the new arrival.

When she saw what it was, she clucked,

A Chick! A Chick!

The hens gathered around to inspect Martha's first child.
"He's very scrawny," said the ginger hen.
"He's very ugly," said the speckled hens.
But Martha didn't give a hoot.
She thought Walliwigs was gorgeous.

Martha spent all her time looking after him.
And Walliwigs thought that Martha was the
loveliest mom in the whole wide world.

"That kid is not only scrawny and squawky, he also eats too much," said the ginger hen to the other hens. "Nonsense," said Martha. "My Walliwigs just has a wonderful appetite."

SQUAWK, SQUAWK, SQUAWK

Walliwigs certainly loved his food.

He ate all his supper.

And every day Walliwigs grew **bigger**,

and bigger,

until Martha's nest was too small.

Martha taught Walliwigs to roost beside her on the perch.

The real problem was—the more Walliwigs grew,
the less he looked like a chicken.
"He's a misfit," said the ginger hen.
"He's not a misfit!" protested Martha.
"He's very special."

I'm somebody special.

But it's not easy being different.

Flat feet! Silly feathers!

Soon Walliwigs began to feel lonely.

Then one afternoon, Professor Beak, an ornithologist who lived next door, said to Aunt Beth, "Do you mind if I take a look at that bird that makes such an extraordinary sound in your backyard?"

When the professor saw Walliwigs, he exclaimed, "How remarkable! I must have it!"

"Help yourself," said Aunt Beth, who had had enough of Walliwigs' funny ways.

But Walliwigs didn't want to leave his mom.

Finally, Professor Beak shut Walliwigs in a special box for carrying birds to the Institute of Ornithology.

Walliwigs squawked and made a fuss all the way to the professor's van.

GGGGGGGGGGGGGa!

Martha was heartbroken. Martha was inconsolable.

Two weeks later a letter from the Institute of
Ornithology arrived for Martha. Aunt Beth read it
in front of everyone.
Well I never!
Did you ever!

My darling Ma,
I am having a lovely time!
The Professor says that I am a
Proposiger aterrimus. That's a special
name for a Great Black Cockatoo. I am
almost an endangered species, so I get
special treatment. I will be getting
married as soon as a suitable bride is
found.

I love you

Walliwigs

Martha was overjoyed. She turned proudly to the ginger hen and the speckled hens and said, "There you are! I told you my Walliwigs was very special."

"Oh, Martha," said the ginger hen, "we would be very honored if you would come up and sleep on our perch."

"Yes, yes, do please join us," clucked the speckled hens . . .

. . . but Martha was much too busy planning
something wonderful to wear for the wedding.